·GOLDILOCKS·
AND THE THREE BEARS

REWRITTEN BY MADGE TOVEY
ILLUSTRATED BY SUZANNE SMITH

Once upon a time, there was a family of bears. Papa Bear was big and gruff. Mama Bear was middle-sized and sweet. Baby Bear was very small, with a squeaky little voice. They lived in a snug house in the big, dark forest.

One morning Mama Bear made porridge for breakfast.
"This porridge is much too hot," she said in her sweet voice.
"Let's take a walk while it cools."

Off the bears went into the big, dark forest.

Soon a little girl named
Goldilocks came to the house.
She knocked on the door. Nobody
answered. "Oh, dear," she said. "No
one seems to be home. But this is such
a cute little house. I'll just look inside."

The first thing she saw was the table with three bowls of porridge.

"I'll just have a taste," she said. She took a sip from Papa Bear's big bowl. "Oh! This porridge is too hot!"

She tried the porridge in Mama Bear's middle-sized bowl. "This porridge is too cold!"

She tasted the porridge in Baby Bear's tiny bowl. "This porridge is just right!" she said, smacking her lips. "I'm going to eat it all up!" And she did.

Then Goldilocks went into the parlor. She saw three chairs.

"I'll just sit down and rest," she said. She tried Papa Bear's big chair. "Oh! This chair is too hard!"

She tried Mama Bear's middle-sized chair. "This chair is too soft!"

She tried Baby Bear's tiny chair. "This chair is just right!" she said, rocking back and forth. She rocked and rocked until the tiny chair broke into pieces.

Goldilocks picked herself up. "I'm so tired," she yawned.
"A nap would be nice." She went upstairs and found three beds.

She tried Papa Bear's big bed. "Oh! This bed is too hard!"

She tried Mama Bear's middle-sized bed. "This bed is as soft as mush!"

She tried Baby Bear's tiny bed. "This bed is just right!" she said with a sleepy sigh. "I'll just lie down for a minute."

Goldilocks closed her eyes. Before she knew it, she was fast asleep.

Very soon the hungry bear family came home. They sat down at the table.

"Oh! Somebody's been eating my porridge, too!" gasped Mama Bear.

"Somebody's been eating my porridge, and it's all gone!" squeaked Baby Bear.

"Somebody's been eating my porridge!" growled Papa Bear.

The unhappy bears went into the parlor.

"Somebody's been sitting in my chair!" growled Papa Bear.

"Oh! Somebody's been sitting in my chair, too!" gasped Mama Bear.

"Somebody's been sitting in my chair!" squeaked Baby Bear. "And it's all broken into pieces!"

By now the bears were very upset. They rushed upstairs.

"Somebody's been sleeping in my bed!" growled Papa Bear.

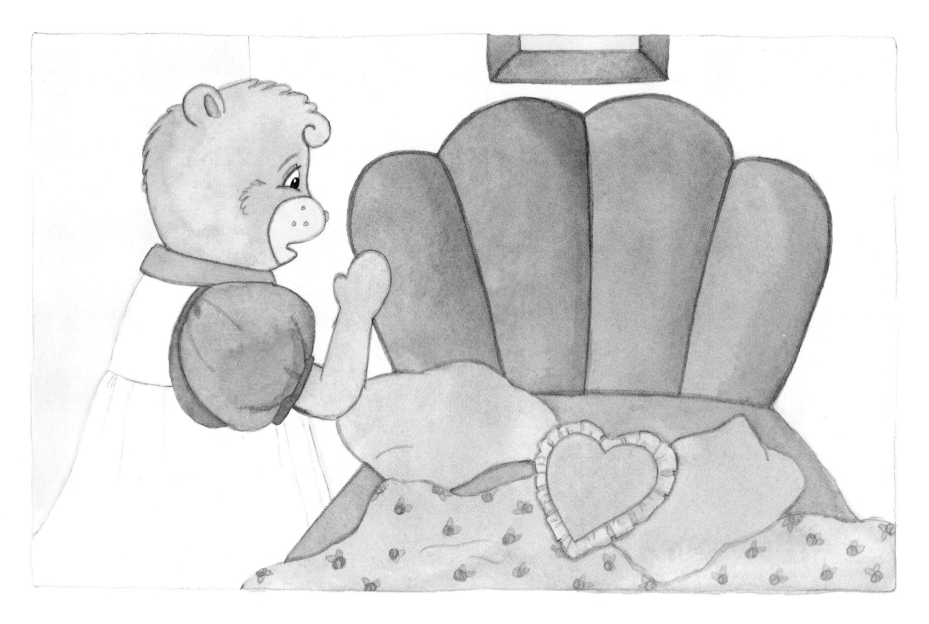

"Oh, dear! Somebody's been sleeping in my bed, too!" gasped Mama Bear.

"Oh!" squeaked Baby Bear. "Somebody's been sleeping in my bed!
And here she is!" Baby Bear's squeaky little voice woke up Goldilocks.
When she saw the three bears, she jumped up like a frightened rabbit.

Before the bears could stop her she raced down the stairs,
rushed out the door, and ran for home as fast as she could go.

And the three bears never saw Goldilocks again.